The Greatest Gift Series

12 Lives Changed
By Jesus' Birth

By

Jonathan Srock

D1566560

If you enjoy this book, please visit my website and subscribe to my email newsletter.

Signing up gives you the free gift of my short story collection.

Every month you'll be updated on my blog and everything that's happening.

Thank you for your support!

Visit https://www.jonathansrock.com/ and subscribe

Copyright © 2019 Jonathan Srock

All rights reserved. This book or any portion thereof may not be reproduced or used in any manner whatsoever without the express written permission of the publisher except for the use of brief quotations in a book review.

All Scripture quotations and references are the translations and paraphrases of the author.

This is a work of fiction. Names, characters, businesses, places, events, locales, and incidents are either the products of the author's imagination or used in a fictitious manner. Any resemblance to actual persons, living or dead, or actual events is purely coincidental.

Cover Photo by Gerd Altmann from Pixabay

Printed in the United States of America

Jonathan Srock
87 Safe Harbor Lane
Smithmill, PA 16680
srockenator@gmail.com

www.Jonathansrock.com
www.solidrock831.com

Acknowledgments

I'd like to thank everyone in my writers group at The Write Practice for reading these stories and giving me much valuable feedback to make them even better. These authors and writers include Tina Weaver, Jane Bolton, Ryan Benson, Mike Van Horn, Gwennie Dysinger, Kenneth Badoian, Regi Amieva, Rebecca Lea, Georgiana Marshen, Melanie Daniels, T. L. Reigns, Joslyn Chase, Evie Haskell, Karen Crawford, and Shujen Walker.

I also gave this book to my beta readers who pay valuable information and encouraged me. My readers include Matthew Niebauer, Elismar Rodriguez, Magevney Strickland, Marvin Nemitz, Linda McDonald, and Beverly Srock.

Thank you all for the hours of reading, critiquing, proofreading, and editing. May God bless each of you for your labor of love.

Table of Contents

Introduction

Every year since I was born my immediate family gathers either on Christmas Eve or Christmas Day. Before we open any gifts or do anything else we read the Christmas story from Matthew 2 and Luke 2 of the Bible. I know that there are millions of Christians who do the same thing or go to a Christmas Eve service where the story of Jesus' birth is recounted.

But for many, because they have heard the story so often during Christmas, the greatest story ever told loses its glory. It becomes mundane, a ritual Christians practice out of religious motive. The Bible becomes just another book, a book of faith, but just something we read out of custom.

One of my goals as a minister is to bring the Bible alive by showing the history and culture through the stories I tell. As I recount the Christmas stories, I see the greatest gift in Jesus that humanity could ever receive. We must never forget the reason Jesus came and the extraordinary events and people surrounding his birth.

I want to recapture the wonder and awe of these prophetic events that Jesus fulfilled on that wonderful night. It was just the beginning of his soul-saving mission. Join me as I attempt to reopen the imagination, reignite our joy and wonder at God becoming man to pursue his rescue of fallen creation through fictional, yet historical and cultural accuracy.

Incarnation

"Son, I'm thinking of giving them free will." The Father sat on his throne as they met together, one of countless meetings between them. They thoroughly enjoy their time together.

"But you know what this would mean..." The Son made eye contact with his Father and the Spirit. They exchanged glances momentarily before he continued, "He will not hesitate to make his move. You know how jealous he is."

The Father chuckled to himself, "Indeed. He's been trying to steal my throne since the beginning. The only way he thinks he can hurt me if he can't take my throne is to destroy my creation, to rip it from me and taint it with his stench."

The Son sat back in his chair, "Even more than giving him an open door, we must form a plan to win them back after he has done his worst." A knowing glance passed between the three.

"I have already been thinking about it. But before we talk about this plan, we have a job to do." They stood and began their work. The Father started with a booming voice, "Let the heavens and earth come forth!" Sweltering fire and hot lava burst everywhere and exploded, spreading in every direction. Any observer would not be able to tell any part of the creation from the rest of it. It was a hot mess!

The new creation began to cool, spheres of molten rock with rivers of white-hot plasma crawling between the spherical bodies. The Spirit hovered throughout the creation bringing stability to the chaotic mess. All types of heavenly bodies took shape. Stars emerged, forming galaxies beyond measure and number. Magnificent planets, stars, nebulae, and galaxies beautifully hung throughout the universe.

Then the prize of creation could be seen far off, a small rough marble still cooling. Father and Son gave it their full attention and worked on their pride and joy. They had incredible plans for this tiny planet. The whole drama of history would play out on this stage.

The Spirit hovered over the waters of the earth continuing to bring order to the chaos. As the Father spoke all things into existence, the Son worked with him to produce what he spoke. When it came time to make the pinnacle of his creation, God formed the man out of the dust and breathed life into his nostrils.

He put his personal touch on humanity. Then He spoke everything else into creation. But with humanity, he got his hands dirty. His great care for these human beings would cost him and his Son more than anyone could imagine.

Soon after they completed creation and rested from all their works, they continued discussing the plight of humanity. The three gathered together in the throne room once again. The Father explained how they would win their creation back. "He will overplay his hand without realizing it. But the road will be hard and long." His face looked graver and graver as he spoke.

"How can we help?" The Son knew the Father did not want to follow through with the plan he had in mind. "The enemy will take full advantage of our love for our creation. He will use it against us."

The Father looked at his Son, nodded, and continued, "That is why I am sending you. Spirit, you will start the process. There is a young maiden I have been watching since she was born. She is righteous, exactly the kind of person I can use. She will make a great mother for my Son, humble but willing to step out. She doesn't care what others think when she knows she pleases me."

The Son smiled, "She seems like the perfect person for our plans. If only there were more like her that yielded themselves to our will. How would the Spirit make a way for me?"

The Father beamed with pleasure, "He will overshadow this young maiden with his presence, providing the perfect space for you to enter her and begin to grow. That's right; we are doing the impossible again. You will become a human being, part of creation. You will feel everything they feel and experience human life to its fullest. When you save the world, no human will be able to say you don't understand what they're experiencing."

"Wow! They will never understand exactly how we are doing all of this. They will spend millennia trying to figure it out. I love it!"

The Father seemed to visit a place of intense pain for a moment. "But there are many drawbacks to this plan. It is the most costly attempt we can make for their hearts, but it comes with extreme suffering. You will be separated from us, a separation you have never known. A time will come when I will not be able to look at you. You will take on the whole world's sin.

"Like an alchemist, you will change their sin into righteousness through suffering and dying in the worst way humanly possible. I will have to watch you suffer and die. But the benefits are incalculable. Satan will never see it coming. The moment of your greatest weakness when it seems you have lost will be your finest hour of victory."

The Son considered his Father's words. He pondered his hatred for sin because it separated them from the creation they loved and destroyed relationships. There would be times in human history when sin would be so rampant they would consider starting over. The human condition would become much darker before it brightened. But he had an opportunity to save the ones he loved. He made up his mind.

"Father, I am more than willing to take my place in your plan. The cost will be great. But if I don't go, we will lose them forever. The benefits far outweigh the costs. I don't want to be separated from my brothers and sisters. I must do this no matter what it costs me."

The Father understood his Son's resolve but needed to make sure he completely comprehended the weight of his decision. "Son, they won't even understand why you are coming. The darkness will try to overpower you. They will fight you, scheme against you, lie about you, and wash their hands of you. You will be dying for people who hate you."

"But some will see the light. Those who believe will turn to me, and I will make my disciples great. These believers will see me for who I am and will love me. And I will love these brothers and sisters! Just say the word, and I will go."

The Father stood, approached his Son, and enveloped him in his embrace. "Today, I am a proud Father. My Son and my Spirit will do great things with me. Together, we will take back our creation. We gave them free will so they can choose to love and worship us. Ours will be a genuine relationship rather than Master and robot."

The Father, Son, and Spirit waited for the proper time in history. His beloved human beings would never be the same. They would release their goodwill on their creation. With anticipation, the Father turned to his Spirit and Son.

A tear slid down his face, and he slightly stammered, a slight tremor in his voice, "It is time. I will miss you greatly until your victory and return. Everything is in place. I will miss you while you are gone. I know I will be well pleased with you, my Son."

The Spirit descended to earth, finding the little village of Nazareth in Galilee. He hovered until he saw the place of destiny. The ultimate plan to save humanity would begin in the humblest of towns.

God would fulfill his promise he made to King David long ago. He would order every event and fulfill his prophecies about the tiny town of Bethlehem. David's hometown would become Ground Zero for him to hatch his plan to change the world. His good creation tainted by sin would once again be His people dwelling in his presence.

Prophecy

The morning sun peeked through the clouds and slowly climbed the trees as dawn gave way to day. The people of the small village were already buzzing about their day, selling in the marketplace, elders gathered at the gates, children playing in the streets, and vagabonds scavenging for food and supplies throughout the village.

An old man with a long gray beard slowly approached the town gates. His walking stick slid along the ground as he shifted his weight from side to side, barely lifting up one foot to put in front of the other. While everyone knew of him, no one in these parts was familiar with his appearance. As he staggered along the dusty road, he murmured to himself.

"Oh to hear from Adonia today! What is on your mind, Lord? What shall I speak to these people for you?" He was on a circuit from town to town sharing the Lord's words and visions given to him. The old prophet moved slower than he used to, but still covered quite a bit of ground every day. This little village was about to receive one of the most spectacular promises from God that would ever be uttered.

Upon arriving at the gates, the old man greeted all of the elders. He raised his gaze and bowed toward each one, "Good day to all of you! I come from the east and am headed west, following that beautiful sun today. I've been traveling from place to place proclaiming the Lord's words. How are you all?"

The elder who seemed to be the leader of the pack stood in honor of the prophet, "Greetings, Sir! Have some cool, crisp water. We don't get prophets as visitors here very often. Tell us, what is the Lord speaking to you?" He sat down, leaning forward to hear the word of the Lord. All of his friends also leaned forward, expressing a deep interest in the prophet's words.

As was the custom throughout Israel, the elders stood once again, this time offering their benches to the elderly prophet. He took his seat while they stood to hear what he would prophesy. In Israel, when a rabbi taught, those listening would stand as he sat. One of the elders asked, "What is your name?"

The prophet looked up at him and replied, "Who I am doesn't matter as much as the Lord's message today." He bowed his head, whether to pray or receive a vision from the Lord, the elders could not tell. They waited patiently as they had learned from their youth that good things come to those who wait.

Despite his age, the prophet was skilled at garnering the attention of those around him from years of experience. It was an occupational gift that never left him. He raised his head and spoke, "You know the times and seasons of our nation. Many fear Assyria to our north, but we have no need to be afraid. The Lord sent a sign to us that confirms his promise that this nation will not stand.

"But the Lord has given us a great promise. I recently met with King Ahaz and prophesied the Lord's message concerning our enemies. The Lord promised that within 65 years these enemies will not be a threat. But the King was still afraid and all of Judah with him. He refused to listen to the message of the Lord.

"I told him to ask the Lord for a sign, but he would not even do that! The Lord gave him a sign anyway. This sign confirms the Lord's word that Assyria and their allies will not defeat Judah. And this is the sign: 'Look! A virgin giving birth, and to a son! She'll call him Immanuel. He'll eat curds and honey at the age he knows good from evil. Even before the boy understands good and evil, the Kings to the north you dread will be left to their own devices.'"

The elders around him stood in silence for a moment but then began to whisper among themselves, "Immanuel? God with us? Adonia among us? This thing has never been done! Why should we fear Assyria now? Before he is an adult of 12 years, in only 65 years we will have no northern enemies. But who is this virgin?"

The prophet waited for the chatter to cease before he spoke again, "Only the Lord knows the virgin of whom he speaks. It is likely that King Ahaz is also aware of this young woman. Perhaps the Lord gave the sign to him so he would know which maiden. More important than that is the vision I received when the Lord gave this message to me."

The elders were tickled with intrigue, hanging on the silence until the prophet revealed his vision. Like any master at oratory and dramatic performance, the prophet left a pregnant pause before he continued.

"I saw a young maiden on the back of a donkey, pregnant, along with a man with a walking stick. I recognize the scenery around them and am sure it's outside of Bethlehem. There have been many prophecies about the great King David and this Messiah. I have prophesied about him before. It seems that while this sign is for our generation, its ultimate fulfillment will be in the future!" The men around him pondered the sign and the vision.

The prophet's zeal was palpable as he continued almost uncontrollably, "And that's not all! There are more prophecies and visions about this Messiah. A great light will come upon those in darkness, like the days when Gideon protected Israel. 'Unto us a child is coming. Unto us a son is given. The leadership rests on his shoulders. They'll call him Wonderful Counselor, Mighty God, Everlasting Father, and Prince of Peace. He'll rule with peace and grow the leadership. It will never end. He'll be enthroned on David's throne and rule his kingdom with justice and righteousness forever. The Lord's zeal will make this happen.'"

This time the elders were silent for a while as they attempted to comprehend these two messages together. First, this child is called Immanuel, God with us. Then the four names were all names of God! How would God come and visit them as a human being? Oh to be alive at the time that God fulfills these prophecies completely!

But none of them realized that when God would do these great things no one would suspect he was fulfilling his prophecies. No one would even look at this man as special. That is, until he upset their applecarts. Then they wouldn't be able to take their eyes off of him until they got rid of him. But the prophecies he would fulfill beginning with his birth to anyone who listened and studied them, it would be unmistakable.

The prophet stood up and said goodbye to all of the elders. He proceeded to the gate and began to walk to the next town. When he wasn't traveling, he was writing his prophecies down so they could be remembered. He had no idea that these prophecies about this Messiah would not be fulfilled for 700 years! God revealed his plan to his servants throughout ancient times. When the Messiah came, he fulfilled every prophecy, every jot and tittle written about him. All the ancients like Isaiah could do now is await his arrival.

The Way Home

"One of my heroines is Ruth. I think her story is much like mine. What's your favorite?" Mary worked through the field with her best friend Hannah. They were harvesting wheat by pulling it out of the ground and putting it in their baskets.

"Well, I like Esther's story. There's something about being beautiful, becoming a queen and being used by God to save your people." Hannah kept up with Mary as the two of them continued to work.

As two of the most efficient workers among the women, they always kept each other company. Unfortunately, as they were about to move to another area of the field, they could hear Hannah's father calling them, "Hannah! Mary! It's dusk. Time to go home."

The young women quickly pulled out the last few stalks of grain to throw into their baskets and hurried toward the field's edge. When they came out of the tall stalks, Hannah's father was waiting. "Good work, girls! Let's store these away for the threshing floor tomorrow."

Mary said goodbye to Hannah after they put their baskets away. She set out on the country road for home in time for dinner. The light spring breeze tousled her hair as she walked the familiar path alone. She wasn't afraid because she had done this so many times before.

She always felt safe on her journey to Nazareth. In all of her years nothing had ever happened when she traveled this road. It wasn't like Jerusalem where the streets were full of dangerous thieves and vagabonds.

Everything went along smoothly until suddenly there was a blinding light in front of her. Mary froze in place, flustered for a moment. The brilliant light dimmed enough for her to realize what stood before her.

A glowing being twice her size blocked her way. This menacing giant threatened her way home and her life. She thought hard and fast to piece together everything she was viewing.

The glowing giant was dressed like a warrior for battle, a massive sword attached to its belt. It was covered in a pure white, seamless robe. She finally realized the dead giveaway of two giant wings attached to its back. Mary had come face-to-face with an angel! No wonder people encountering angels in the Scriptures were so afraid.

Her father told her stories about angels but they were nothing like this. The massive angel bent down until its face was next to hers, "Greetings, little favored one! The Lord is with you!"

Mary's face must have been as white as the angel's clothes. She unconsciously clutched the garment wrapped around her head. She was scared out of her mind by its arrival. She was still perplexed about what was happening.

The angel paused and stared at her. It felt like it was staring deep into her soul. It looked quizzically at her and she was afraid it might hurt her. Mary pondered the meaning of this abrupt greeting. Was it her time to die, already?

Her clammy hands shot up to her face and covered her eyes. Nothing happened. She slid her fingers apart slightly and peered between them. The angel blinked at her. She realized it wouldn't hurt her. It had said God favored her.

Perhaps it was not here for God's vengeance. Her wits slowly returned to her as she blinked several times, wondering if this was real. She wanted to pinch herself but figured the angel would not understand.

Seeing the young maiden's fear, the angel spoke again with a booming voice that nearly knocked her over. It waited for another moment before giving the rest of the message. "Mary, God favors you. You are going to have a baby, a son. You will name him Jesus."

Mary looked behind herself to see if anyone else named Mary was following her home. She wasn't surprised when she saw no one, other than herself and the angel. She tried to focus on the message instead of the angel.

The rock-shattering voice continued, "He is the Son of the Most High God. He will be very great. The Lord will give Him David's throne. He will rule Israel forever. His kingdom will never end."

Mary debated with herself if she could ask questions of the angel without something deadly happening to her. She remembered from her father's stories that humans have interacted with angels before.

Out of the stunned silence, her tiny voice asked, "But I am a virgin. How will God do this?" Immediately she put up her hands in defense in case this question went too far. But to her amazement, the angel responded kindly, "The Holy Spirit will overshadow you. God's power will make it happen. Your child will be holy, God's Son."

Mary's mind felt smaller and smaller as she tried to comprehend the angel's answers. Its response yielded a million more questions. What did "overshadow" mean? Was this like the Day of Atonement when the High Priest entered the Holy of Holies to present sacrifices before the very presence of Almighty God?

Was overshadowing like the cloud that formed over the temple? Although she was curious, she felt that asking more questions might anger the angel. She knew she would never fully understand everything God did, so she would trust him and accept it.

As if the angel was able to read her curious mind, it increased her faith with its next statement. "Your relative Elizabeth, who was once barren is pregnant, in her sixth month! Nothing is impossible for God. "

Mary reasoned from this that the same God who could make her barren relative pregnant could also make a virgin pregnant without using natural, human means. She made up her mind to trust God despite how much she didn't understand

She bowed before the angel, "I am the Lord's servant. I know it will happen." The angel smiled at her, disappearing as quickly as it appeared. Mary pondered everything that had happened to her. She was so distracted it was hard to put one foot in front of the other.

When she arrived home, she ran into the house and broke the news to her parents. They took it better than she thought they would. Who can argue with God? Mary decided, rather her parents decided after hearing her story, that she would visit Elizabeth. Her father had the great idea to send her to Jerusalem to help with Elizabeth's pregnancy. Her absence in Nazareth would avoid ridicule when she started to show. It would save her family the humiliation.

The cover story would also protect Joseph. Mary was already pledged to be his wife, an unofficial marriage waiting for Joseph to build their house. People would look down on him for not divorcing her immediately. No one would understand. She would leave the next morning.

But before she left on her donkey, Joseph happened to walk up the street and see her leaving at dawn. She had to tell him what was happening. Maybe if she explained well enough he would not disown her.

"Mary, where are you going?" Joseph was a curious man, but who could blame him?

She cleared her throat and dove in, "I just found out that my cousin Elizabeth is pregnant in her old age. I wanted to go and help her through this time. But I have to tell you something. I sort of met an angel tonight on the way home from the fields."

Joseph's eyebrows shot up on his brow, "Really? That doesn't happen to too many people. What did it say?"

Mary pensively pushed the conversation she was dreading onward, "It told me that God favored me. It said that I'm going to be pregnant with a son and that God would 'overshadow' me. The boy is going to be God's son!"

Joseph stared at her. As comprehension crossed his face, his eyebrows shot down toward his nose. He wasn't an angry man but this kind of news would frazzle anyone, "Are you telling me that you are pregnant, and it is God's fault?"

Mary didn't want to be combative, "I'm only telling you what the angel said to me."

"And I'm to believe that God made you pregnant? What really happened, Mary?"

"I told you everything. I'm not a liar and I don't make these things up."

Joseph put his hand on his head, "The house is almost ready and our marriage is almost official. Everyone is going to ask what I will do with you. Men have disowned women for less. Even more, they will expect to stone you for this." He started turning around to walk away from her.

Mary's biggest fear was becoming reality, "Joseph, please don't go like this. I will be back and we'll figure things out. Don't abandon me now when I need you the most!"

Joseph's arms flailed in the air as if he was saying, "Why? How am I supposed to handle this?" Mary watched his back as he kept walking. Her mother came rushing out to console her but it was too late. The tears poured down her face. She just wanted to get out of town and clear her head.

Mary traveled to Elizabeth's house, and when she entered, Elizabeth's baby leaped for joy in her womb. Without knowing anything about the angel, Elizabeth exclaimed, "Mary, welcome, you and my Lord!"

How did Elizabeth know how special this baby in her womb was? Elizabeth had to explain, "My husband was ministering as priest in the Temple. An angel visited him. But when the angel told him that we would be pregnant at our old age, he couldn't believe it. He questioned if God could do it. Because of his unbelief, God struck him so he can't speak. But when you came in my baby leaped for joy!"

The surprising news helped Mary to see that God can do anything. As she stayed with Elizabeth, Mary helped her prepare for her baby to be born. She was learning everything for her own pregnancy.

The time came for her to go home. But she had no idea what to expect. She could walk into a volatile situation. The town would never accept an unmarried pregnant girl. Everyone would be disgraced.

It would also be impossible for her family. Her father would be disgraced just as much as her. And if Joseph had anything to do with her after everyone found out, he would probably have to move to another town.

She would face everything with the courage her parents taught her to have. This was too big for her to turn back on her word. God would make everything work out.

Panic Mode

"Where have you been?" Mary's father never showed when he was upset. He was one of the hardest men to read. Even after living with him all of her life, Mary still couldn't tell whether she was in trouble or not.

She hadn't realized that her encounter with the angel on the road home had taken longer than she expected. She was sure that a lifetime had passed in her angel experience. It took most of the journey home to get over the shock and realize it wasn't as long as it seemed. Dad always gave her a bit of leeway because she was more responsible than most of his children.

But even that long chain could get very short if he didn't feel she was being honest with him. As much as she hoped she would not have to explain her encounter with the angel, there didn't seem to be an alternative. She gulped and took a deep breath, "Well, I ran into an angel on the way home."

Dad gave her a stern, blank stare, and then burst out laughing. "That's a good one! You really know how to make me laugh." She figured he wouldn't believe her anyway. But she had to try to tell him exactly what happened.

She had always been truthful about whatever was happening in her life. Even though it seemed outrageous, she honestly told him what happened. Her scowl made him stop laughing. He looked deep into her eyes waiting for her to tell him what really happened. All he got was the same honesty and seriousness he always got when she told the truth.

His face became serious again, "You're putting me on, right?" For the first time in her life, he was having a hard time reading her face.

"I really wish I was. I was on my way home as I usually am. A bright light appeared in front of me. Time seemed to freeze and it took me quite a while to realize what was happening. It looked like a giant warrior with a massive sword. I only realized what it was after I noticed the giant wings on its back."

"This sounds just like the stories I have told you since you were a little girl."

"I know. But if it weren't for your stories from the Scriptures I would have had no idea how to react to it."

He searched her eyes once again, peering deep into her soul. A look of concern formed across his face as he realized she was completely serious. He always trusted her no matter how strange her stories seemed, so he trusted she was being truthful now. He sat down so he could take in the situation, "What did it say?"

"I don't think you're going to take it well." She looked genuinely worried about how he would react to the news.

The fear in her eyes seemed to break her father. He was beginning to tear up as he responded, "No matter what it is, we will face it together."

Mary took a deep breath and began to tell him the message the angel had given her concerning being highly favored, becoming pregnant with a Son from the Most High, and the miraculous means God would use. As she relayed the message, her father became more and more troubled. Her pregnancy changed everything about his place in the community.

Mary's mother, Abigail, was listening in the kitchen as she was completing preparations for their evening meal. As Mary was relaying this message from the angel, Abigail came into the room and joined her husband. She also looked quite concerned about Mary's plight. They had always supported Mary in everything she did, but this would destroy not just her reputation, but the entire family's reputation. They would be outcasts forever.

"We have to deal with this gently. You say that our cousin Elizabeth is six months pregnant in her old age? This is amazing! I think it might be a good idea for you to visit her for a while. It will provide a good experience for what you are about to face. It will also give us time to figure out how to deal with this situation. I must also talk with Joseph. This is not something you can hide." Mary's father was always logical in his approach to any problem. She knew he had her very best in mind as he thought out loud about her unusual circumstances.

Abigail nodded as her husband spoke. She had the irresistible urge to stand up and go to her daughter, hugging her for moral support. And that's exactly what she did. Mary was glad for a father who could solve problems and a mother who empathized with her. Because of them, she was righteous and humble enough to be used by God in such an amazing way.

The game plan was set in motion. She would leave the next day to visit Elizabeth. Her father would take care of all of the details in Nazareth. It was a restless night for the entire family, but they all knew that God would lead them through these troubled waters. After all, he chose Mary for a reason and would not let her flounder about without his guidance and protection.

At the first sign of sunrise the next morning, Mary had already packed everything she needed, said farewell to her parents and family, and mounted her donkey. But then the worst thing that could have happened came walking up the street.

Joseph waved to Heli, Mary's father, "Heli, I could use your help in my shop today." Then he noticed Mary on the donkey.

"Where is Mary going so early in the morning?"

Mary's parents looked at one another and then Mary. Even though her father was supposed to explain what was going on, Joseph blew that plan up. Mary lowered her face, "Joseph, I need to talk to you." She looked at her parents and they got the hint. They grabbed her siblings and scurried off into the house, having no problem letting her deal with the situation.

They watched through a window as Mary spoke to Joseph for about two minutes. He became more and more perturbed with every word. He was a pretty even-keeled man but he didn't stick around very long after her explanation. He said something quietly to her and then turned and walked away.

Mary was visibly shaken, the tears flowing down her face. Abigail ran to Mary but there was no consoling her. Her father also came out to see her. "Can you make the trip alone or should I come with you?" He really didn't want to spend the day in the shop with an angry Joseph.

Even though Mary was sobbing, she was a strong woman, "No. I can do this. God picked me because he knew I could do it."

Her parents wished her farewell and safe travels once again and the donkey plopetty-plopped down the town street. Mary's mother and father carefully considered all that must take place in the short three months before her return.

Heli went into the house and prepared to go to work with Joseph. "If only I could take a sick day today," he muttered to himself. He came out to the main room, kissed his wife, and headed to work. Instead of opening his own shop today, he would be working with Joseph. He walked into the shop and stepped into the back room. Joseph was hammering away at one of his projects for a patron.

He decided to speak before Joseph, "How much did she tell you?"

Joseph continued to hammer away. Then he stopped, and the silence was killing his future father-in-law. Finally he responded, "She's pregnant and I know it's not mine. She's going away to her cousin for a while."

The air turned stale. Before Heli could speak again, Joseph asked, "How long will she be gone?"

"Three months."

A slight smile formed on Joseph's lips, "In a way, that's good. That would give me enough time to finish the house. That is, if I decide to formalize the marriage."

Heli didn't know what to say. He wanted Joseph to give Mary a chance. "Did she explain how she got pregnant?"

Joseph met his gaze for the first time, "Yes. But it doesn't make any sense."

"Believe me. Her mother and I don't understand it any better than you do. Why would God do such a thing?"

"I'm still not convinced of her explanation. But I have never known Mary to lie to me or be deceptive in any way. I think I just need some time to sort it out."

"If it helps," Heli said, "she informed us that her cousin Elizabeth is pregnant in her old age. It's almost like Sarah's story from the Torah. If God can do that, he can do anything."

Joseph didn't seem enthused, "Congratulations. I know God can do all things. I just don't understand this."

Joseph surprised Heli with his next request, "What would you do if you were me?"

Heli stood there for a while, trying to figure out how to respond." If I were you, I would be upset and disown her. It seems too far-fetched."

Joseph hung his head, "I'm surprised you would say that about your own daughter."

"I know. But I want to be honest with you, as I have taught all of my children to be. I don't think she's lying. She's never lied to me before. I love all my children no matter what happens to them."

Joseph looked up, "I greatly respect Mary. That's why I wanted to marry her. But I have a lot to think about in the next three months." He paused and then continued, "Just in case I decide to stay with her and go through the coming storm with her, do you mind stopping by the house and helping me with it tonight?"

Heli's eyes filled with hope, "Of course. Speaking of projects, what do you need my help for this morning?"

"I have a Gentile client who has some interesting designs in mind. I need a hand holding everything in place while I make measurements and cuts and piece it together."

The two men worked completely in silence other than the noise of their tools. Their friendship was tested today, but remained intact for word

The Close Call

Tomorrow was a big day for Joseph. As he lay in his bed waiting for the dawn to arrive, he considered the massive project he had to finish today. How would he ever get it done? A Gentile friend decided to take him on after seeing some of his best work. But then, the skilled project he gave Joseph was at least a two man job.

He tossed and turned, writhing over the decision. "Adonai, my Lord, what am I going to do? Mary and I could really use this money to finish the house and start our new life. But I can't finish it on time. What can I do?" He waited but didn't hear anything.

After about an hour of sleepless indecision Joseph felt the peace of the Lord coming over him. Suddenly, he felt an intuition. Of course! How did he not see this already? He had been discussing Mary with the Lord but forgot that her father was an experienced carpenter who could help them do the work. All he had to do was see if her father, Heli, could spare a day to help him finish the work.

There would be no sleep for Joseph now. He immediately jumped out of bed, washed his face in his basin, and proceeded to get dressed. The faster he got to Heli the better. Joseph hoped he would catch him before he opened up his own shop. Joseph didn't want Heli to open up and deceive his patrons by having to close up shop to help.

Skipping his usual breakfast, he bounded out of the house and headed over to Mary's house. He figured he would eat breakfast when he returned after securing Heli's help. As he raced through the tiny streets of Nazareth, he dodged a few sellers who were already displaying their wares. He almost took out an entire cart of figs but managed to stay on his feet. "Sorry! Sorry!"

He was almost out of breath as he approached Mary's house. But as he looked up, he noticed that Mary was on her father's donkey. Where would she be going at this hour? Something had to be wrong for Mary to be doing this so early in the morning. But he couldn't help enlisting Heli's assistance first.

Jonathan Srock

He slowed to a walk, sweat pouring off of his brow. "Heli, I could use your help in my shop today." He peered up at Mary for a moment and asked the awkward question, "Where is Mary going so early in the morning?"

Heli and his wife stared at one another, then looked at Mary. Joseph didn't think it was that hard of a question. Mary hung her face in shame. He wasn't used to seeing this from the woman he loved. In the tiniest voice she had ever used, she responded, "Joseph, I need to talk to you." She glanced at her parents and they scurried into the house with all of their children.

She made eye contact with Joseph, tears in her eyes. Joseph couldn't help seeing her tears. "What's wrong, my love?"

"Something happened to me last night on the way home." The look in her eye told Joseph Mary was still grappling with how to tell him. "On my way home I saw an angel and it told me I will become pregnant and be the mother of God's Son."

Joseph was stunned. He didn't even know how to react to this bombshell. For what seemed like an eternity he stood before her speechless. And then his face contorted with anger, "Whose child is it?"

Mary's face turned white and he thought she might push him away. When her arm shot towards him, he braced for impact. But it was Mary's gentle touch, "I haven't been with any man. God is doing this. It's a sign from God. Who else could make a virgin pregnant?"

Joseph was incredulous, and rightly so, "You expect me to believe that God made you pregnant last night on the way home from work?"

Mary tried to console him, "Joseph, my dearest, I understand you are angry with me. But could you think about how I feel?"

Mary paused and then continued, "I am going to see my cousin Elizabeth. The angel told me that my cousin Elizabeth is pregnant in her old age. Can you believe it! It's a sign from God that he can do this too. He can make a virgin the mother for his holy Son."

Joseph barely heard anything she said. Nothing she could say would change anything. Their lives became more complicated than ever. He and Mary were legally pledged to one another. Even though the marriage wasn't completely official and consummated yet, they were in the process, too far to turn back.

He knew he had two options. He could disown her publicly as he should. She'd be considered an adulteress and, what hurt Joseph's heart even more than her betrayal, she would be stoned to death for her sin. He could barely stomach the thought.

The other option was to take her as his wife. They would be looked on with scorn for the rest of their lives. Forget about a business. He would never work in this town again. He would never be able to provide for Mary or a son that wasn't his. By the time he finished the house to take her in, she would be showing.

Joseph felt like an animal backed into a cage ready to strike. But he also loved Mary so much. He didn't want to yell at her or cause her any problems. It's too bad that society didn't leave a third option to save face. But that's not how the law worked. It was too harsh for this situation.

The more Joseph thought about the situation the less he had a plan to deal with it. Unfortunately, his frustration came out. He didn't mean to aim it at Mary, but she was the only one there. He waved his arms more wildly and dramatic than he realized, "What am I going to do with you? What are we going to do? We are pledged to one another!"

Mary didn't say a word. She just sat on the donkey and took the barrage of hurtful words from Joseph. The moment he had the outburst, he regretted it. But it couldn't change what just happened. The problem with words and actions is that you can't take them back once you use them.

In shame, he wanted to retreat to his shop to work, while he thought about the problem, or go home and take the day off and forget about the project that would set them up for success in life. What success could they have now?" He didn't realize he was walking away from the love of his life, and he didn't even look back.

He barely heard Mary sobbing on her donkey. He just kept walking, keeping his mind busy. Otherwise, he would lose it for sure. He decided to go back to his house. He walked in the door kicking the frame. Why did God have to do such strange things? The Scriptures said that he could do all things. But why would he do this?

In his heart of hearts, he was afraid that she was covering something up. But at the same time, there was a sliver of hope that the humble and righteous woman he fell in love with was still there. Then it hit Joseph that he was going to be working with her father all day today. If the situation could get anymore awkward, he had no idea how.

Joseph was too out of sorts to eat his breakfast. And he forgot his lunch as well. Nothing else mattered until he figured out what he was going to do. He had until Mary returned to make his decision, inform her and her family. The best thing to do right now was go to work and use the hammer to pound out his frustration.

***

Joseph managed to show up at his shop on time. He gathered his tools beginning work on the big project he needed Heli's help to finish on time. He pounded away at the wood with his hammer. Every once in a while carpentry provided the perfect place to cool down, even though he was not an angry or violent person.

It wasn't long before Heli came into the back room of the shop where Joseph did most of his work. He had no idea how to break the ice. He just kept hammering away, this time a little more in control of his emotions.

Heli almost shouted so Joseph could hear him, "How much did she tell you?"

Joseph finished pounding the nail into the wood, then stopped. The silence hung in the air. He couldn't think of what to say. He blurted, "She's pregnant and I know it's not mine. She's going away to her cousin for a while." All he could do was state the new reality of his life with Mary.

He had to make a decision about their relationship, so he asked Heli, "How long will she be gone?"

He waited for a moment when his future father-in-law answered, "Three months."

A wry smile kissed the corners of his lips, "In a way, that's good. That would give me enough time to finish the house." He paused for a moment, "That is, if I decide to formalize the marriage."

He could hear Heli breathing hard, "Did she explain how she got pregnant?"

Joseph turned around meeting his future father-in-law's gaze, "Yes. But it doesn't make any sense." Joseph still couldn't wrap his mind around the whole situation. He knew it was possible for God to do anything. He just couldn't understand why God chose Mary.

But then he thought about it for a while. If God was going to choose someone to be the mother of his Son, Mary was the perfect choice. For all the reasons he loved Mary, her humility, her righteousness, her kindness, she would be a great mother. He was almost lost in his thoughts about Mary.

Heli responded, "Believe me. Her mother and I don't understand it any better than you do. Why would God do such a thing?"

Joseph could understand how Mary's parents felt. He was in the same boat. But nobody can comprehend God's reasons for his actions. He still had so many doubts and spoke out of his emotions, "I'm still not convinced of her reason. But I have never known Mary to lie to me or be deceptive in any way."

He could hear a slight uncertainty in Heli's voice, "If it helps, she informed us that her cousin Elizabeth is pregnant in her old age. It's almost like Sarah's story from the Torah. If God can do that, he can do anything."

Joseph felt like he was hanging over an abyss. On the one side was his understanding that Mary did something immoral and he had to figure out how to deal with it. But on the other side, her story was not far-fetched. God had done all kinds of strange things in the Scriptures.

His voice sounded more deflated than he wished, "Congratulations. I know God can do all things. I just don't understand this."

Even though he wasn't sure what would happen, Joseph knew he had to prepare in case all of this was true. There was no way he could abandon Mary to walk this road alone. His love for her could surpass their circumstances.

Joseph felt like he needed guidance. He had always looked up to Heli and so he decided to ask, "What would you do if you were me?"

Heli's voice sounded deflated, "If I were you, I would be upset and disown her. It sounds too far-fetched."

Joseph couldn't believe his future father-in-law's response. That was not the answer he expected, or wanted. He hung his head, "I'm surprised you would say that about your own daughter."

Heli's voice shook, "I know. But I want to be honest with you as I have taught all of my children to be. I don't think she's lying. She's never lied to me before. I love all my children no matter what happens to them."

Joseph was beginning to see that he was asking the same questions Mary and her parents were asking. He tried to be hopeful as he raised his head, "I greatly respect Mary. That's why I wanted to marry her. But I have a lot to think about in the next three months."

He paused and then continued, "Just in case I decide to stay with her and go through the coming storm with her, do you mind stopping by the house and helping me with it tonight?"

He could see Heli's eyes brighten, "Of course. Speaking of projects, what do you need my help for this morning?"

"I have a Gentile client who has some interesting designs in mind. I need a hand holding everything in place while I make measurements and cuts and piece it together."

The two men worked completely in silence other than the noise of their tools. Their friendship was tested today, but remained intact for now.

***

That night everything changed. Joseph laid down for an unsettled sleep. The third time he sought rest, he got a surprise. Suddenly in his dream, a giant celestial being appeared to him, glowing brighter than the sun with huge wings protruding from its back, and dressed for battle in armor with a giant sword.

Before he could react in fear, the angel called his name. "Joseph, son of David, don't be afraid to take Mary as your wife. The Holy Spirit is using her to bear God's Son. You must name him 'Jesus.' He will save his people from their sin. Isaiah proclaimed this long ago, 'Behold, the virgin will bear a son, Immanuel.'"

Joseph awoke in a cold sweat. He immediately believed Mary, after seeing the angel. His mind was made up. He would be obedient to do what God told him to do.

The next morning, he stopped at Heli's shop, excited to tell him what happened. He told his father-in-law that he was fully committed to the marriage. He couldn't wait for her to come home.

***

After an agonizing three months of waiting, Mary finally returned. He met her at her parents' house and recommitted to their marriage. "Mary! Mary!" She turned to face him, a noticeable round bump on her belly.

Her face fell when he looked at it. "You look beautiful!" He rushed to her side, pulled her close, and gently lifted her chin. Then he gently pushed her face upward to lock eyes with her. He put his hand on her belly, "And you will call his name Jesus."

Her jaw dropped as a look of recognition crossed her face. "How did you know?"

"A giant angel told me! I don't care what anyone else thinks. I want to be on this journey with you."

Mary hugged Joseph with a huge smile on her face. The road would be difficult, but she didn't have to worry about doing it alone.

***

Almost six months later, the Roman government demanded with a new edict that everyone take a census. Both Joseph and Mary belonged to the house of David. Joseph would have to go to Bethlehem at a crucial time in Mary's pregnancy. But Mary refused to let him go alone. As much as she knew the trip would be hard on her, she would not be alone.

Joseph couldn't deny Mary. They would register as husband and wife when they got to Bethlehem. He promised her that they would not consummate their marriage until after Jesus was born. They would walk this rough journey together. Neither of them would allow anything to get in the way of God's plan for Jesus.

No Room for You

I was making money hand over fist in our little town of Bethlehem thanks to some politicians. Like any other Jew, I wasn't fond of any of them. The great Roman Caesar Augustus demanded a census be taken of Palestine. All I could think was that they just wanted to take more taxes. It would be such a pain in our small town. So many Jews would be returning from all around the Empire. We wouldn't be able to hold them all.

Although Bethlehem is a tiny town, it was the home of King David. The moment the census was declared, everyone had to return to the place of their lineage. Bethlehem became flooded with all kinds of people. We had Jews from other places in Palestine.

But there are a number of people who settled in other parts of the Roman Empire. Jews from the far reaches, outnumbered by many Gentiles in their homelands. I can't tell you what a joy it was to see them visit. There's just something about being in the majority that makes you feel more connected to your people.

My little inn barely turned a profit for most of the year. But it became a cash-camel overnight! So many people were looking for a place to stay during the census. My inn filled up at the beginning of the first night.

Every business in Bethlehem was booming. I thought right away about all the money I could have made if I had expanded my inn. My wife reminded me I'd backed out of tearing down the stable and building more rooms. Oye vey, I should have listened to her.

As the sun was setting I worked hard to accommodate all my guests. I was so busy I almost didn't hear the slight knock at the door. When I opened it, there was a man with his very pregnant wife standing before me. I immediately thought of my wife when she was pregnant with our children.

Despite the long travel and discomfort from wherever in the Empire they came, his wife was radiant even in pregnancy. They seemed to be down-to-earth people, but they needed a place to stay. And I had no room left.

I really felt for them, but I had to disappoint them. I had no rooms left. I opened my mouth to release the devastating news, "I'm sorry but I have no more..."

The husband desperately interrupted me, "Please, sir! My wife is already in labor. We have nowhere else to go. There are no other inns with rooms. You are the last person who can help us tonight."

"I told you, sir, I have no more room. My inn was one of the first to fill up. I sympathize and wish I could help you," I told the man and his wife. I didn't want to be the bad guy, but I had to turn them away. I felt terrible about it, but there really was nothing I could do. The man looked so sad and distraught.

Then the husband made me feel even worse, "Sir, we've been traveling for over two weeks from Nazareth in Galilee." I felt that pinch in my gut as I roughly estimated the over 97 mile journey. I thought of my wife's pregnancy again. There is no way I would still be alive if I took her on such a long trip in this condition.

As I watched them slowly walk out of town, he lovingly and carefully made sure his wife was as comfortable as she could be. Suddenly, I remembered a slim possibility for lodging they might consider. I ran as fast as I could, shouting after them, "Wait! I have another option!"

The husband turned around when he heard someone yelling his way so late at night. He stopped the donkey she was riding and waited for me to arrive. I huffed and puffed as I caught up with them, realizing how out of shape I am. I immediately suggested, "The place we store the animals, there may be room in there for you. It's not comfortable or made for people at all, but it's all I have to offer."

It was a terrible idea, and I would've never stayed there. I was struck by this couple's response. I expected them to rake me over the coals for even offering such a place, but they smiled warmly and began thanking me profusely. I helped them on their way back to the stalls where guests' animals stayed.

The husband told me his name was Joseph, and his wife was Mary. They had recently been engaged, but Joseph was still building their house. In our culture, the husband builds the house during the legal engagement so that the wife can move in and they can begin their marriage together.

Because it was a big taboo for a legally engaged couple to already have a baby on the way, I didn't ask any questions. It was none of my business why she was already pregnant. They were the kindest people, and I wish I had better accommodations for them.

Once Mary settled in the barn, I ran into the inn to see if I could find anyone that could help. This baby was coming tonight, and very soon. After dashing into the inn, I immediately asked, "Does anyone here know how to deliver a baby?" A couple of women stood up and told me they have helped with deliveries before. We were blessed!

After the midwives saw the situation in the barn, they ran into the inn to get the proper supplies. Poor Joseph was doing everything he could for Mary, but he was out of his depth. As soon as the other women returned, I grabbed him by the shoulders and pushed him out of the barn. I sat down on the ground while he paced back-and-forth.

That's when I noticed the brightest star I had seen in a long time in the heavens. It looked like it was hovering right over my barn! In fact, it seemed like a beam from that star was shining directly on the barn. I had never seen anything like it before. "Joseph, do you see that star?"

Joseph looked up as a pointed to it and weakly responded, "I'm really not surprised. You probably wouldn't believe me if I told you everything that's happened so far."

I didn't want to intrude but now I was curious. Joseph started telling me all of the events that took place in the last few months.

After hearing everything he and Mary went through, I was sure the star was a sign to somebody, " I believe your little one may be an extraordinary baby!"

As I pondered the meaning of everything Joseph told me, one of the women called for him, "Joseph, come and see the baby. He and Mary are ready!"

***

I was just a lowly innkeeper but even I knew that anything in the sky when the baby was born meant they were significant. Adonai, my Lord, keeps an interest in babies that will change the world somehow. I don't profess to know much about these matters but I've heard of them happening with children born for his unique purpose.

Like anyone about to become a father, Joseph didn't even register that I was speaking to him. He just kept pacing, mumbling prayers like any father-to-be might do. I didn't know what else to do for him and remembered my own nervousness when my first child was born. I could sympathize, but men don't really do that.

We waited for what seemed like hours, but the baby came quickly. We heard that signature cry and knew the baby was here. Joseph sprinted into the barn to meet the new member of his family. I followed him in and saw a baby wrapped in swaddling clothes and lying in one of the mangers.

It was an ironic experience. Here the special baby boy lay in a manger, a feeding trough for camels and donkeys. It seemed the last place you would find the King of the Jews, as we would later discover. And yet his presence in the manger reminded me that humility is a precious gift.

There was an unmistakable awe as we watched the infant smile at Mary, his eyes darting around the barn, staring at all the animals. The light from the star shown through the door and Mary was glowing. They named him Jesus, an unusual name that means, "The Lord saves." As the midwives and I went back to the inn to give the family some privacy, we saw shepherds arriving to see the baby.

Joseph and Mary stayed at the inn for a couple of months after that night. The star followed them wherever they went. It's not every day an inn keeper like me gets to be part of the historical things God is doing through babies marked for his greatness, like this one. I couldn't help but keep up with the couple, after they left my barn.

I discovered that they ended up staying in Bethlehem for a while. I looked them up visiting from time to time. About two years later King Herod, the most paranoid and corrupt politician we've ever had, found out about some royal infant to be born in Bethlehem. He sent soldiers into Bethlehem to protect his throne.

That star I noticed during Jesus' birth drew some Magi, wise kings, from the East who wanted to worship him. King Herod wouldn't stand for this at all. The soldiers murdered every boy two years and younger, very close to Jesus' age. I was anxious for Mary, Joseph, and Jesus, but I didn't need to worry at all.

Joseph and Mary were careful not to tell too many people that they took Jesus and left Bethlehem quickly before the soldiers came. It appears God was watching over them. Shortly before they departed, I heard through the grapevine that some kings from the East came to visit Jesus. This was the talk of the town for several weeks. This family was blessed by God and, although I don't know where they went, I know their story is unlike any other story I have told in all my years.

Inviting the Nobodies

The men gathered around the campfire that cold, dark night. They were considered the lowest of the low in society, dirty, smelly men that no one wanted to be around. That is, until it came time for an essential ingredient in Israelite life to be tended. It was sad that they got such a bad rap because their job was crucial.

The Passover Feast in Israel was the busiest and most profitable time. Everyone bought a lamb for their special dinner. You couldn't celebrate Passover without one. But beyond job security during that season, some of the greatest men in Israel, great leaders everyone admired, started out as shepherds. King David was a shepherd before he was king. Moses was a shepherd before God called him to lead Israel to the Promised Land.

Shepherding was one of the hardest jobs in Israel. Today, almost everyone of the shepherds lost at least one of their sheep. One shepherd lost his sheep to a bear while another lost one in the wilderness. He tracked it for three hours. Sheep were their livelihood but they also cared for them.

He finally found it trapped in the thorny thicket and brought it back to the pen. He gently put salve on every wound. This was a thankless profession. Although everyone wanted their lamb for Passover, no one cared to hear how it was kept safe all of its life.

Shepherds were humble people who did their job well without complaining. They didn't care what people thought of them. As they sat around the campfire, they exchanged stories for entertainment as they warmed themselves, shared meals together, and kept watch over each other's flocks. They had shepherding down to a science, putting all of the sheep in caves and pens hewn out of rock and hills around them.

One of the shepherds pulled out a lyre and plucked the strings, playing a hearty tune for his friends. The others listened and hummed along, some lightly clapping their hands. After a stressful day of dealing with ornery beasts, chasing down wayward sheep, and providing medical care for those caught in briars, this was their downtime. A few would be chosen to guard the sheep pens while others would enjoy their sleep.

As they enjoyed one another's company the night wore on, and many of them were getting very tired. Just as they were beginning to stand up and bow out for the night to get some rest, the skies filled with bright light. Curious, they all looked up to a brilliant sight. A giant glowing angel with huge wings appeared before them, its seamless white garments flowing in the wind and giant sword clinging to its hip.

The entire group of shepherds hit the ground, some kneeling and others laying prostrate, out of complete fear. The angel began to speak to them! To them, the nobodies of Israel. Why would an angel think it was worthy of their presence? As they shook in terror, the angel tried to calm their nerves, "Don't be afraid!"

Of course, it was too late for that. A few of the shepherds recovered quickly, and were able to get to their knees. Looking up into the heavens, they watched the angel as it continued, "Pay attention! I have great news for you, and not just you but everyone. Tonight, in Bethlehem, David's city, a Savior is born. He is the Messiah, the Lord. But don't take my word for it. I have a sign from God. You'll find a baby wrapped in swaddling cloths and lying in a manger."

Before the shepherds could even comprehend what the angel was proclaiming, a host of many angels filled the night sky! If it was even possible, the heavens exploded with light as a congregation of angels began to proclaim, "Glory to God in the highest, and on earth peace among those with whom he is pleased!" As suddenly as the angels appeared, the night sky was now as dark as it was before they arrived.

The only bright light left was an unusual star they had not noticed before. Eventually, the other shepherds joined the ones still awake in the fire pit. They sat in silence for a few minutes and then began to speak to one another. One could be heard whispering, "Who are we that we should see angels?"

Another whispered to his friend, "What are we going to do now?" There was much confusion throughout the camp of shepherds. No one had ever relied on them to make big decisions or leave their posts for anything. But this invitation could not be ignored because of those who gave them the message.

If there was anything any of them had learned about the Scriptures, you did not ignore the appearance of an angel. They made the decision to go and see the Christ child, their long awaited Messiah, despite the mandate to not leave the sheep unattended. They trusted that God would take care of the sheep while they were gone.

When they arrived in Bethlehem, they like he told everyone on their way to the barn about what the angels had told them, what they had seen and heard. They were the first to spread the word of the miracle of the birth of Christ. Then they arrived at the place where Jesus was, passing the owner of the inn and a couple of women along the way.

They quietly entered the barn and saw the baby wrapped in swaddling cloths and lying in one of the mangers. The sign the angels gave them was confirmed. They couldn't believe they were a part of this precious moment. These humble shepherds were given the first invitation to the most important event in all of human history to that moment.

One of the shepherds spoke softly, "This is a holy moment. See how this great king lies in a humble manger? Those are only used to feed the animals. Now they are the crib of a mighty king! It makes me feel welcome that he comes into the world so humbly. This good Shepherd started out humble like us."

Each of the shepherds bowed in awe in front of Mary and Joseph and the baby. The infant smiled at his mother Mary and father Joseph. He seemed to be the happiest baby in the world. Joseph told them the baby's name was Jesus. What a beautiful name! There was a miraculous sense in the air as the light from the star they had seen above the barn shone through one of the windows.

Those in the same profession as the great leaders of Israel like Moses and King David were given the opportunity to see the Good Shepherd first. Not only was this the Good Shepherd, but he would also be the Passover lamb slain for the sins of the world. It was as if God planned to welcome the king of the universe into the world in the humblest of ways and invited the humblest of men to see their King first.

They came into the room as quiet and reverent as possible, almost as if they were entering the sanctuary of the temple. It was a gentle, tender, and holy moment. Approaching the manger, each Shepherd bowed and shrunk to his knees. They had nothing to offer this newborn King. But someone who has angels inviting you to their birth is someone who is going to do something unusual in Israel.

Mary picked up baby Jesus and cuddled him in her arms. The shepherds knew they were in the presence of greatness. Mary and Joseph walked up to them and began to speak with them about how they knew the baby had been born. The shepherds recounted the story about the angels appearing in the heavens as they were just going about their typical night.

Mary's gentle spirit continued to be a calming presence for the child. She looked like she had been a mother for many years even though this was the first few hours of her motherhood. Joseph was curious as well. He was stunned that angels would invite the shepherds to come and see their baby.

Joseph and Mary told their story to the shepherds, who were beginning to see God's hand in everything that was happening. The baby stayed nuzzled in his mother's arms, sound asleep. The star the shepherds observed in the sky and followed into town was still over the barn. They were surprised that no one else had been invited or was aware of the strange signs of the star and this baby in the manger.

They began to ponder why God would have the Messiah be born in a barn. To them, humble beginnings didn't fit the station of the Messiah. And yet it had the telltale signs of the kind of thing God would do and has done in the past. In a way, it made sense that God would do things this way.

They longed to stay with the baby and his beautiful family all night, but they had responsibilities back in the fields. So they reluctantly said goodbye to the father and mother taking their last look at the historical baby. They left the barn to journey back into the fields. As they went back through Bethlehem, they told anyone they saw about what had taken place.

Entering the fields once again, they found the sheep safe and sound, and everything in its place. God had rewarded them for being obedient going to see baby Jesus. They settled around the fire, no one able to sleep after the events of the night. There was much talking and celebrating around the fire.

Every Shepherd was full of thanksgiving for being chosen to see the event of human history. They glorified God and praised him for what he was doing in Israel. They had no idea that the Messiah would be much more than just the Savior of Israel. They were wired and knew that they would be up all night. But that didn't matter. There have been sleepless nights before in this profession. But this one takes the cake.

Celestial Privilege

It had been centuries since the cosmic war between Lucifer and Yahweh. The angels that joined Lucifer were cast out of heaven forever. They serve him now but, the roughly two thirds of the angels that did not side with him still serve Yahweh today. That was the last big thing that happened in the universe as far as we angels were concerned.

Being an angel in heaven is the assignment of a lifetime. Serving Yahweh is the very best job any angel could ask for. We are involved in many of his plans. Most of all, we enjoy observing what God is doing throughout his creation on a regular basis. Only a couple of us are known to humanity.

Michael is the archangel and a great warrior. He leads the armies who fight for the Lord of Hosts into battle anytime they are needed. Michael is the most capable military commander anyone could ever ask for. More than that, he has never lost a fight. No one wants to call the cosmic battle with Lucifer his glory days, but every time he goes against him, he's unstoppable.

Another one that the humans have known in the past is the Angel of the Lord. I must be careful in calling him an angel because the Son sometimes embodied this Angel of the Lord when he wanted to visit human beings in person before it was his time to fulfill God's secret plan for his creation. We knew he was somehow involved with a plan formulated before he created the universe. But that's much higher than my pay grade.

When the Son wasn't involved in visiting humanity as the Angel of the Lord, one of us would use this term. We had to be very careful because when one of us would appear as the Angel of the Lord, humans would be in great fear and bow before us. When the Son was not the Angel of the Lord, we would quickly stop them from bowing down before us. We are not God even though we may be scary at first sight.

That's the problem, we must remember when we visit earth. We are so used to being huge, mighty warriors that we often forget how fearful they can be of us at first sight. After all, most of us are ready for battle at any moment and are quite taller than almost all humans. The only ones that could remotely compare to us were the Nephilim, those humans that resembled giants long ago.

I am one that is known to some humans as well now, especially after the most significant role of my life in being a chief messenger for the Lord of Hosts. I remember that day like yesterday. We don't often get called into God's throne room, and many of us enjoy being there to worship him in his many facets. Believe me, being on worship duty is the best assignment any of us ever get.

The Lord informed me that I would announce the arrival of the Messiah! That secret plan I mentioned earlier was about to be executed. And I was blessed to be his herald to proclaim to the human beings what God was doing. I was so thrilled I almost lost all decorum in the midst of the throne room!

As I knelt before the throne trying to contain my enthusiasm, Yahweh outlined my role in his plans, "Gabriel, first, you will go to Mary. She will be one of the most important servants you will ever meet. She is humble and kind, the perfect mother for my Son. You will proclaim to her my plan formed from the beginning of the ages."

I dare not interrupt as Yahweh spoke, but I cannot contain myself any longer. I burst out, "Mother for your Son?"

There's a reason Yahweh is God of the universe and not me. He didn't even show that he was perturbed by my outburst. He smiled, "Yes. You are the first other than the Son and Spirit to know. And I chose you for this mission because you are one of the most articulate angels in my service. I am going to do the impossible yet again by sending my Son to become a human being. He will save them from their sins and open the door for me to be reunited with my fallen creation."

I was stunned. How simple, and yet elegant and profound this plan must be. I know Yahweh wouldn't tell me everything he's doing, but I sensed he was going to lay out my part in it. I was surprised that Yahweh chose me above all the other angels because I tend to ramble. I would really have to bring my A-game when I fulfilled my role for him.

He leaned forward in his throne, "Gabriel, you will be my messenger. First, you will speak to Mary and tell her that she will bear the Son of God. She will ask you how this will happen because she's a virgin. You may give her this answer: 'The Holy Spirit will overshadow you.' She will want to know more, but she will choose to trust me and will not ask further.

"Then, I am sending the Angel of the Lord to speak with her husband, Joseph. He will want to divorce her quietly because of her situation. It will be up to the Angel of the Lord to give him my message that he must not be afraid to take her home as his wife despite this unusual situation. He will make an excellent father for my Son on earth.

"Then I want you to lead a host of angels in the skies outside Bethlehem to the shepherds. They will be the first to meet my Son. Like them, he will be the Good Shepherd his believers will follow. He will also be the ultimate Passover lamb who will offer the final sacrifice, forgiving people for their sins restoring the relationship between humanity and me.

"You will be joined by a host of angels after you proclaim the good news of my Son's birth in Bethlehem and tell them about the sign of him wrapped in swaddling cloths lying in a manger. You will be immediately joined by a multitude of angels proclaiming glory to me because of salvation in my Son."

"Thank you, Lord, for this great opportunity! I will do my best in your service." I was dismissed from the throne room and couldn't wait to prepare myself. First, I thought about what I would say to Mary. Then, I tried to remember that humans weren't used to us and would not react well. I needed to remember to say, "Do not be afraid."

I thought about what I would say and rehearsed to make sure I would get it right. Then I heard my friend, the Angel of the Lord, being called into the throne room. We were both getting the roles of our lifetimes. I was so excited to be considered for these assignments.

It was just about time to visit Mary and tell her the good news. I headed down to earth and looked for the tiny village of Nazareth. It took me a while because I underestimated how small Nazareth really was. I finally saw Mary on a country road outside of the village. When I swooped down in front of her, I couldn't contain my excitement no matter how much I had rehearsed. I don't even think the beginning of my message registered for her.

That's when I remembered to tell her not to be afraid. It was probably way too late for that. I left her some time to regain her sanity and then relayed the rest of the message to her. Just as Yahweh said, she asked how this could happen. I answered the way the Lord instructed me. She was struggling to learn more but decided not to pursue the matter anymore. I wouldn't know how to respond if she did ask.

When I got back to heaven, I considered the mission a success. Except for a small oversight, I accomplished everything I was sent to do. I now prepared for my second role as the lead for the shepherds. I had six months to get ready. When the time came, I found myself back in service to Yahweh. This time he sent me to another small town, Bethlehem. Just outside the city of David, I located shepherds sitting at a campfire after a long day's work. I entered the atmosphere but forgot again how much humans are afraid of angels. They dove to the ground as I showed up.

I keep forgetting that humans don't see angels very often. But I recovered again. "Do not be afraid" seems to be my go-to opener. Then I told them the great news, that the Christ was being born in Bethlehem. I gave them the sign and queued the heavenly host to appear. We glorified God for what he was doing in human history.

It's a privilege to serve God and be available for whatever he wishes. I have seen so many things in service to Yahweh. But I was most honored to be chosen as God's spokesman to Mary and the shepherds. There is nothing like being on mission for God. Angels are always at his beck and call, and we were created for this purpose. I will never forget being God's messenger at the most crucial time in all of human history.

Risk and Reward

The two kings met one another in King Nabu's palace. As they sat down in the throne room, the first started the conversation, "My dear friend, Belshazzar, you will not believe what my scholars have come across."

King Belshazzar raised his eyebrows, "And what, may I ask, have they found, Nabu?" One of the fascinations among Babylonian kings was to discuss scholastic quandaries and astronomical phenomena.

King Nabu responded, "One of my astronomers has found an irregularity in the stars!"

King Belshazzar raised his right eyebrow, "Please don't keep me in suspense."

King Nabu continued, "I have already summoned my astronomers to tell us all about it." He waved his hand and a couple of the servants opened the massive doors to the throne room and announced his astronomers to the court.

Ten astronomers walked into the room and bowed before the two kings. King Nabu spoke to King Belshazzar as if they weren't in the room, "My chief astronomer will share the news with us." He raised his index and middle finger in an upward motion and the first astronomer before him arose. King Nabu introduced him, "This is my best astronomer, Sumai. He hasn't been wrong yet." Then the king called on him, "Sumai, tell us what you told me earlier."

He stepped forward and responded, "My King, we have noticed a star in the West. It showed up in the last month and has remained constant. It does not move as the other stars do. We believe it's a sign signifying an unusual phenomenon. This is all we know."

King Belshazzar turned to his friend, "How can we know what this means?"

King Nabu stroked his beard for a moment in deep thought and then replied, "Perhaps one of the prophets would know what it means."

"To discover this, we should call on our friend Adini. He is the one with all of the prophets and scroll scholars." The suggestion seemed good, so they immediately sent for their friend. "We know it will take him and his scholars eight days to travel. Let us meet together then."

Eight days later the three Kings met once again in Belshazzar's palace. King Adini greeted his friends, "I see you've been having a party without me!" The others greeted him with warm hugs.

King Belshazzar responded, "You were always the partier." All three kings burst out laughing. A third throne was brought for King Adini, and they proceeded to sit down and talk.

King Nabu opened, "My astronomers have recently found a sign in the heavens, a star that rests in the West without moving. We have come to the conclusion that this sign may be linked with a prophecy in the ancient scrolls. We thought it might pique your interest as much as ours."

King Adini sat back and pondered the information. Then he leaned forward toward his friends, "This is interesting indeed. When your messenger brought your request to meet and gave me an idea of the topic, I thought it wise to bring my best scholars with me. They like digging around in the minutia of matters." He called one of the royal servants and told him to bring his chief scholar.

The chief scholar entered the giant throne room and bowed before the three Kings on their thrones. King Adini gave him his assignment, "We are curious to know how the ancient prophecies elaborate on the strange celestial sign of the bright star in the heavens. Collaborate with the astronomers and search the scrolls. Then come and tell us what you have found."

The scholar bowed his head, responding, "We will need a few days to search all of the scrolls and find this information. We will report to you as soon as we have discovered everything to know about this." The king nodded and raised his hand to excuse the scholar.

The chief scholar immediately assembled the team and they searched their scrolls concerning the star. Although they were efficient, this took several days because there were many scrolls. It turned out that the kings would have to wait five days to hear any discoveries from the documents.

The Kings enjoyed the time by having a small feast party. Then in five days, King Adini summoned the scholars to hear their report. The chief scholar approached him with two scrolls.

The first scroll contained the prophecies of a Hebrew prophet who lived in Babylon in the times of Nebuchadnezzar, roughly 500 years ago. It prophesied that there would be a King called the Messiah, or "Annointed One." This King would save Israel in some way.

The second document described interstellar signs from that land throughout the 500 years astronomers have been studying the heavens. There were some indications by different astronomers that this Messiah may have a star that would follow him when he was born. The kings' excitement was evident as they discussed the issues. "You know, my friends, we must go and meet such a King and bless him," King Belshazzar could barely contain his excitement.

King Nabu joined in, "We must follow this star and find out what it means."

King Adini concurred, "Even if our scholars are wrong, my wife wouldn't mind having me out of the palace for a while." The others chuckled as they confirmed their wives felt the same way.

King Nabu spoke up, "It's settled then. We'll follow the star until we find whatever it is resting above. We should form a caravan and prepare some gifts in case it is this Messiah."

A few days later after completing the preparations, the caravan containing the kings, their servants, supplies, and close friends of royal lineage departed toward the West. It might take years to reach their destination, but they decided the risk was worth the effort.

The most treacherous part of the trip was passing through the desert. The perilous journey could end in the midst of the sands. Getting lost was easy, but the star guided them West. Water supplies were a constant concern.

They had expert knowledge on managing water supply. Camels didn't eat or drink much. They knew where every watering hole was located, as well as retaining condensed water in the cold night.

After many months of travel, they passed the desert, and from there could travel more efficiently. It took nearly two years to reach Palestine in the Roman Empire. They arrived in Jerusalem, Israel's capital city, and sought King Herod. They figured one of his sons was this Messiah.

King Herod informed them he was unaware of any King. His one favor asked of them was to tell him everything they learned about this King's location, and when they first saw the star. He claimed he wanted to worship him as well. They agreed to return after finding him giving him the information on the baby's possible age.

They followed it until arriving in Bethlehem, at the house of Joseph and Mary. They entered and found Jesus, now about two years old. The kings and royal officials presented their gifts to the child. The chief gifts were gold, frankincense, and myrrh, all fit for a king. After a couple of days in the village, they said their goodbyes.

As they were on their way back to King Herod, Adini was suddenly struck by a dream and fell off his camel. His friends dismounted and rushed to him. After the vision, he stood up and said, "Friends, I just had a vision! We cannot trust King Herod. We must go back a different way."

King Belshazzar responded, "Who are we to ignore the gods? I know another way." The caravan rode away from the sunset. It would take them many months, if not years, to return home. But every step was worth seeing the Messiah who would deliver his people. Little did they know, he would save the entire world.

Paranoid Protection

In my opinion, it's the toughest place to rule. Nobody does you any favors by sending you to Palestine, especially to Judea. Only a top-notch king can rule that place, especially if he's not Jewish. Like any other ruler in the Roman Empire, I had to make sure no one would steal my throne. Were there days I didn't think it was worth it? Never!

At least the king gets to control every aspect of life in his kingdom. I was no different. I knew the Hebrews would never be satisfied with anyone but a king that was chosen the way they were used to picking them back in the day. I wasn't Jewish, so I had to make sure no one would replace me.

The throne must be guarded, but not with my life. I protected my rule with the lives of those who wanted to steal it. Anyone could be called into question. No one was above reproach. My wives seemed to always have it out for me, but I took care of that. So what if I'm a widower. I prefer to say I'm single.

You must be wary of any family member because your relatives can challenge you for your throne. My own sons seemed a little shifty to me, so I had them murdered. That took care of that. After all, Alexander and Aristobulus wouldn't have been acceptable kings anyway.

But there are family members you can trust, distantly related, unpopular, and unfit to rule. The best tactic to maintain control in Judea is to fill the Sanhedrin with family members. The Sanhedrin was the ruling religious body, and I made sure they did my bidding when it came to this paramount aspect of Jewish life. I gave them a little bit of power to keep them away from any idea of taking my throne.

But the best way to protect your throne in Israel was to give the Jews gifts in one hand and raise taxes with the other. The right gift brings gratitude while they pay taxes. Ever since their return from the exile, when they rebuilt their temple, it was a lackluster, small space compared to the former glory of Solomon's Temple. I heard that when the older generation saw it built in their day, they wept. But I fixed that. I built up the Temple Mount and expanded the temple, decorating it with my extravagant flare. Instead of weeping over it for a puny replacement, they danced in the streets.

If you make them happy, you can pull any shenanigan you wish. I made one of my best Babylonian friends the High Priest. The funny thing is, the High Priest is supposed to be Jewish! But as I said before, put the few people you can trust in these positions to rule for a long time. I also kept filling the office of the High Priest with Egyptians.

When you know everyone's after you, you have to take all of these steps. I even made a standing army that was on my side. You never know when there's going to be a revolt in Israel. They happen regularly. To make them happy, the army was made up of both Jews and non-Jews.

After all of these steps to protect myself and my throne, I didn't see the Messiah coming. The tradition of the Messiah comes mostly from ancient Hebrew prophets. In a time when the Kings of Israel were not carrying their weight, the prophets began to prophesy about the ultimate king who would save his people.

The only reason I found out about this threat was through some good friends – at least I thought they were good friends – from the East. They arrived one afternoon and asked which of my newborn sons would become king. They wanted to worship him and give him gifts. Red flags! I didn't have any sons that young.

Paranoid to the heavens, I started thinking of any possible sons I could've had lately. Nope. There were none. I called in scholars to discover any prophecies that proclaim this idea of a Messiah. They were quick to inform me of predictions about a Son of David who would sit on his throne forever. I wasn't having any of that.

One of them quoted the prophecy, "The Messiah will be born in Bethlehem. The prophet Micah tells us, 'But you, Bethlehem in Judah, not least among rulers. A great shepherd comes from you for Israel."

This struck me to my core. My paranoia was on overload, and I was terrified. I had to find out everything I could to stop this threat. I went secretly to my visitors, "My good friends, tell me what you know of this Messiah."

One of the kings gave me the whole story, "One of our astronomers saw the strange star in the sky, and we combined his discovery with recorded prophecies and signs. An old Hebrew prophet exiled to Babylon named Daniel prophesied about this Messiah, calling him the Son of Man. The star had been in the sky for about two weeks before our caravan left. That was almost two years ago."

Now it was time to set the trap. The Kings wanted to keep talking, but I found out what I needed to know. I was polite, "My friends, this is magnificent! When you find this Messiah child, you must come back and let me know. I too will go and worship him! I know the Hebrew people have been waiting for centuries for his arrival. They will all be so pleased."

Another king from the East responded, "Yes, Herod, we will certainly do this. Let us depart so we may find him. Then we'll return and tell you so you can also do the same." With that, they left to do my dirty work for me. If there was anything I excelled at as a king, it was making sure all threats were eliminated.

I waited for days and days without any response from these kings. They were nowhere to be found in Jerusalem or the surrounding areas. That was the last straw! If they didn't help a fellow king maintain his rule, I would do it myself. Do you remember that standing army I created? It was time to use them.

I gathered them from the barracks and gave them their mission, pacing from side to side, "If you haven't heard already, there is a threat to our kingdom. Hidden away somewhere in Bethlehem is a child who will usurp my throne. We must neutralize this threat immediately. Go to Bethlehem and search for every male child two years old and younger, and slaughter them before he has a chance to rule."

I thought I heard groans among my elite soldiers. I stopped pacing and stared them down, "Who groaned? Be a man and show yourself." No one moved. I walked between the ranks and every head was pointed forward. No one diverted their eyes. Then I noticed three soldiers looking down at their feet.

I casually walked over toward them. They kept looking down. When I stopped in front of them, they would not look at me. I had found my dissenters. "You three, follow me to the front of the lines." When we arrived at the front, I decided to make an example of them.

"Did you question the orders of your King?" Nobody answered. I yelled, "Do you question the orders of your Sovereign?" They were becoming more and more uncomfortable, shifting weight from foot to foot.

One finally got the courage to open his mouth, "Your Majesty, I have three boys at home. My oldest is three. My youngest was born two months ago. I cannot in good conscience kill boys that are my own children's ages."

I responded, "I see. So you would allow some illegitimate child to take over the kingdom that has been so good to you?"

He was on the defensive, "No, Majesty. But can't we just imprison them?"

I stomped on his foot and punched him in the stomach. He doubled over, "You are not the King. You are a servant of the king."

He stood at attention even though he grimaced, "I wish to be excused from this assignment, my Lord." I heard the other two agree under their breath. I would have to make an example of them.

"Very well. Is there anyone who wishes to join these three?" Not a single soldier came forward. I excused them and they turned their backs to exit the barracks. I pulled out my own sword and stabbed all three in the back. They crumpled to the floor never to undermine me again.

As I wiped the filthy blood off to clean my blade, I stared at all of my soldiers again, "Are you ready to carry out your mission?"

The soldiers stood at attention, "Yes, your Highness!" Then they proceeded from the barracks toward Bethlehem. I sat on my throne waiting for the news that every two-year-old and younger was dead. Finally, my messenger entered informing me of their success. My throne was safe.

One of the prophecy scholars requested a hearing, and I readily granted it with curiosity. He entered, bowed before me, and pulled out a scroll. Without a word of introduction, he read, "In Ramah, a voice. Weeping and deep mourning. Rachel is weeping for her children. She won't be comforted. They are gone forever." Although I didn't excuse him, he turned around and left the room. Scholars have thick heads and are very rude.

I didn't care if I fulfilled some prophecy by protecting my throne. As far as I was concerned, I would reign as King forever on this throne. Sadly, despite my efforts to remain on my throne, I found out later that the Messiah will be an eternal king.

I also discovered that no matter what I did to keep my throne, it would not be enough. I soon became very ill with painful cramps, crumbling pain in my lower back that would be my downfall as I faded into history. I would only be remembered as the paranoid King Herod, Butcher of Bethlehem, who ultimately failed to stop the Messiah.

Meeting the Messiah

Many long years I have waited for God's promise given me to become a reality. I visit the Temple daily, praying and hoping that the day comes. The Lord has told me I will see the day the Messiah arrives, the Savior of our people. From my youth, my parents have encouraged me, "Simeon, you will be a great scholar someday. Pour over the scrolls every day and don't forget the Temple as many scholars do." I have studied the Scriptures, even more zealously now that the Lord has promised such a great thing to me.

From scroll to scroll, God has outlined the Consolation of Israel, the saving of our people. The Scriptures I studied in-depth talk of a Messiah figure who will save Israel, right the wrongs to my people. I can't even describe what it is like to wait this long.

Many prophecies have been given concerning this Messiah. God has told me I will not see death before I see him. Each day I awake in hope, and it hasn't come yet. But I don't lose heart. If the Lord has said it, it shall be!

I have lived in Jerusalem all my life. My favorite time of year is during the three great feasts, the Feast of Booths, Passover and Pentecost. I love these feasts because of the many sojourners that visit the city in awe of what they see. You should see their wide eyes and gaping mouths as they gaze at the temple, or when they offer sacrifices in the courts.

I fear that living here for so long opens the door of familiarity with the things of God. This is dangerous because you can get too comfortable with God. I've learned over the years that the moment you think you understand God, he surprises you with a new facet of his being. Arrogant people think they have God figured out. Humble people approach him in awe cherishing every revelation from him. I seek to know him in his overwhelming presence.

Some around here consider me mad because of my learning. These people say it has all gone to my head. But that is not true at all. Much of it has also gone to my heart. Besides, it's not only about studying the past and the Scriptures. I feel that when I pray, God responds to me, and I listen to him. I believe him when he says I will see the Messiah.

Trusting in a God who has always been faithful pays off. Today I wake up and feel God's Spirit telling me today is the day. My curiosity is getting the best of me. I'm too excited to eat breakfast. I decide to go to the temple. Sure, I do this every day, but today it feels like I should be there early.

Walking through the bustling streets of Jerusalem never gets old. Everyone from merchants selling their wares to scholars arguing about the law, to children playing in the streets, and even the poor begging on the sides of the road, all part of the background noise surrounding pedestrians. I finally arrive at the Lord's temple.

As I walk into the court of the Gentiles, where anyone can meet and pray, buy sacrificial animals, and offer sacrifices, I decide to get away from the crowd noise and enter the court of Israel, the second inner court of the Temple where only Israelites can meet. These two courts are separated by a wall warning Gentiles their lives are forfeit if found beyond it. "Gentiles" are all of the people from other nations. Unfortunately, many of my people look down on them because God revealed himself and his law to Israel first.

I sit on one of the benches and watch the crowds. Then I see them. A husband and wife with a newborn boy. I sense this is a holy moment, and I feel the nudging of the Spirit of God. I've often felt the Spirit as I've worshiped in the Temple but I feel him stronger today. A yearning inside, a still small voice pulls me toward this couple. If I don't step out now, my opportunity to meet the Messiah will never happen again. My heart pounding in my chest, I stand and walk up to them as casually as I can.

Nervously waiting for their dedication ceremony to end, I try not to look awkward standing to the side. A dedication ceremony happens eight days after the baby is born, as parents dedicate the child to God through circumcision to be recognized as part of God's covenant with Israel. If I'm right about this boy being the Messiah, that priest has no idea who stands before him.

My hands are shaking in anticipation, but also here because I have never been so bold in all of my many years. The parents turn toward me to leave, but I step out in faith and trust this new feeling from the Lord is right. My heart leaps through my chest, and my stomach is at my feet. "Excuse me! May I speak with you privately?"

Both parents turn around abruptly, both with wide eyes and raised eyebrows. Then they nod their heads and follow me to one of the rooms where people study the Torah. I can barely control my nervous energy as I sense that moment again. "I overheard the priest name the boy Jesus, meaning 'The Lord saves.' Did I hear correctly?"

His parents don't seem nearly as nervous about me as I thought they would. If I knew better, I would think they've been experiencing many strange encounters like the one in front of them. His father is gracious, "That's correct. And my name is Joseph." He gestures toward his wife, "His mother's name is Mary."

I smile cordially, "May I hold him?"

His mother nods again, "Of course."

I take baby Jesus in my arms and, suddenly feel a surge of electricity, which I know to be God's Holy Spirit coming upon me. I lift the boy in my hands toward the heavens, "Lord, now I can die in peace. I've served you and your Word many years. But now I look upon your Salvation prepared in the peoples' presence. He is a light revealed to the Gentiles and for glory in Israel."

Everyone studying the Torah in our room, and even some passing by, look at me like I'm an old madman. I don't care. I've found I can get away with almost anything. People just think I'm eccentric. But in Israel, they still have to honor their elders.

I lower him and then return him into his mother's arms. His parents' faces are aglow with wonder. I try to explain as best as I can, "I have been waiting for many years to meet the Messiah. The Lord promised me I would see him before I died. Now I can go in peace."

They marvel at my words. I can see his mother is deep in thought, considering my words, almost as if she is memorizing them, writing them on her heart, like the new covenant, to remember and quote them later.

I bless both parents, knowing they have quite a journey ahead of them. As more and more people discover his true identity, much change is coming, not just to Israel, but to the world.

I feel the Lord speaking through me once again. I turn to Mary and speak softly, for it was only a word for her, "Pay close attention. God has made this child that many will fall and rise in Israel. Many will oppose his sign." Then I lean in and whisper in her ear, "A sword will also pierce your heart." As his mother, Mary must know that people will persecute the Messiah as he tries to expose their motives. She would be at the front of the pain they would cause him. I finished speaking what God's Spirit told me, "Many hearts, thoughts and intentions, will be exposed."

Joseph confides in me, "You know, Jesus is very different. We've had many confirmations of this from the moment he was born, and even before that. He already has quite a story, and you just added to it."

I thank him profusely for allowing me to meet Jesus and pray God's blessings upon him and his parents. They thank me walking out the door into the cold, dark world. They seem like the perfect parents for the Messiah. My day is complete, and my mission accomplished. These are events I will never forget but will take with me to my grave..

Fulfilling the Promise

My favorite story from the Scriptures is Hannah and Samuel. As a prophetess myself, I like the story of the first prophet of Israel. That was way back when they called them seers instead of prophets. How exciting it must've been to walk with some of the greats like Elijah, Elisha, Isaiah, and Hosea!

I love that story because Hannah was willing to give up her only son after waiting so long to become pregnant. Then she turned around and gave that son to the Lord, consecrated him to service in the temple! Her dedication to the Lord is much like my own.

I have led a blessed life in the Lord. I married my husband at the usual age and enjoyed seven years of marital bliss with him. But then the biggest tragedy of my life struck. My husband was conscripted into King Herod's army. For a while, I enjoyed the lifestyle of a military wife, like Bathsheba.

In a riot put down by Herod's army, my husband was one of the casualties. I was told he died bravely with my name on his lips. I miss him so these many years. Phanuel, my father, began picking out new suitors for me but I decided to never marry again. He was not very happy at all. "Anna," he asked me, "who will take care of you if you don't take another husband?"

In our culture, a woman cannot take care of herself. They think she must have a male provider. If it's not your husband, it's your father or brothers. I began going to the temple so much out of comfort after his death that I became attached to it and quickly made the decision to dedicate myself to prayer and fasting, worshiping the Lord every day in the temple.

I am now 84 years old! The years seem to go by so quickly. I don't feel that old. Perhaps serving the Lord all my life has kept me young. Besides, age is just a number. I discovered early on that I had a particular gift for hearing from God and prophesying. Female prophets are unusual, but that's what began to happen. Not too many male prophets have been too happy about it. But I let God speak through me.

Although it took a while for rabbis and other prophets to recognize my gift, once they saw that the Lord was using me, they respected it. The prophetic gift can be hard to explain. Sometimes, it comes upon me suddenly, and I don't even realize I'm proclaiming his words. Other times, it's almost as if he's giving his words to be written down or spoken several times over to different people.

I was praying in the temple one morning, as I usually do, when I felt the Lord prompting me that we had an extraordinary guest. I couldn't believe what he told me next. The Messiah we've been waiting for ages to come to us had finally arrived! He was here as a baby with his parents. Today was his day of dedication.

I must admit that I became very excited. I could barely contain myself and asked the Lord if he would point him out to me. Then I began walking around the temple in the different courts waiting for the Lord to show me which one was the Messiah. There weren't too many dedications of firstborn males that day. But any of the priests could perform such ceremonies.

It was a very busy day, like most days. I was in the outer court of the Gentiles for a while, hoping to see parents with a newborn baby. No such luck. But I did get jostled about by people who wanted me to be out of the way. As much as elders are to be respected in Israel, it's not as true for women. Many don't view women with respect, especially so go down to pick me of the youngest men.

One particular beast of a man actually knocked me over, turning to me and looking down at me laying on the floor, "I didn't see you there." He chuckled as he walked away. He didn't even help me up! What if I broke a hip? No matter. I got up on my own brushing myself off. I have learned to be an independent woman.

I went to the court of Israel next. None of those rude Gentiles from other nations would be allowed past the wall that separated the two courts. A big sign warned them that they were not allowed past it on penalty of death. That'll show them. In the court of Israel, I was treated with a little more respect.

The Messiah child could have been anywhere. If I weren't in prayer for the guidance of the Lord, I probably would've never met him that day. But, the Lord was with me and blessed me with the opportunity to meet him personally.

I couldn't help myself. I told everyone I saw, "The Messiah is here! The Lord has told me he has come to save us from our sins! Never forget this day, because it is the day of our Salvation. The one prophesied about to save us has come!" Most of the people I proclaimed this to probably thought I was just some insane woman. If they ignored me, it was to their own peril.

I was so excited that I may have gone overboard in my presentation. I probably looked like a crazy lady, but sometimes my zeal for the Lord and his message gets ahead of me. After all, I'm not the craziest prophet in the group. You should hear some of the others. God uses prophets of all shapes and sizes as his mouthpieces. Of course, there's always the serious ones as well. Prophets are all different, just like all of God's creatures.

I ran into my good friend Simeon and couldn't resist telling him about the Messiah. To my surprise, he told me the Lord was already speaking to him about this child. He said God promised him he would meet the Messiah before he died. We agreed that whoever saw him first would tell the other. We parted ways so that we could find him before we missed the opportunity to meet the most important person in our history.

I continued to evangelize about the Messiah's arrival to anyone who would listen. Multitudes of people visited the temple daily. That's why it took so long to discover which one was the Messiah. As I combed through the people to try to find him and his parents, I noticed Simeon talking with a married couple holding the baby.

I asked the Lord if this was the chosen one. As he confirmed that these were the Messiah's parents, I patiently waited outside the room for my opportunity to meet the Messiah. I tried to give Simeon space, but this was the Messiah, a once-in-a-lifetime opportunity!

After I heard Simeon making his proclamation about the Messiah, I tried to stroll into the room casually, but that didn't fit my personality. What seemed to me to be casual strolling might look like running to everyone else. I couldn't resist any longer. I rushed into the room like the waters of the Jordan River. Some people say I have a lot of nervous energy. I prefer to use the word "enthusiasm."

Within seconds, I was right beside Simeon. I forgot to introduce myself as I usually would with, "Hello! My name is Anna. I'm not crazy." Instead, I simply began to prophesy about the child, "This child is the Messiah! The Lord has been waiting for many centuries to deliver this gift to his people. He will save them from their sins but at great cost. May you be blessed as you raise this child and prepare him for the path he must choose. The way will be made straight for his journey."

The parents shocked me because they did not look surprised at either Simeon or me. The mother seemed to be taking all of this attention in and storing it away in her heart to contemplate later. The father smiled warmly at both of us while telling us their story. The events he described seemed like those found in the Scriptures about other great leaders in Israel. I knew that what the Lord spoke to me was confirmed. I will never forget for all of my days that I got to be part of the greatest epic ever told.

Dear Reader,

Thank you for taking the time to read my book. I appreciate your support and hope that you enjoyed fictional stories about how it may have been during the time of Jesus' birth.

There's another way you could continue to support me. One or more of these actions will give this book more visibility or connect you to everything I'm doing:

- **Please leave a review.** If you go to the place you bought the book and leave a review, whether good or bad, this helps the book to be more visible in the marketplaces. This is a quick way to support both me and this book.
- **Please sign up for my email list.** If you are interested in following me or engaging with me more, you can go to my blog at www.Jonathansrock.com and sign up for my email newsletter. You'll get some free short stories and be emailed anytime I release a blog or news.
- **Please like my Facebook author page and share my books and posts.** Type "Author Jonathan Srock" in the Facebook search box. You'll get even more news about my activities. Also, you can share this book and other resources by me in your social media feeds.

You can always contact me through my blog at https://www.Jonathansrock.com or my email address (srockenator@Gmail.com). I hope to hear from you!

Blessing,
Rev. Jonathan Srock

About the Author

Rev. Jonathan Srock is an ordained minister with the Assemblies of God for 10 years. He received two Bachelor's degrees in Biblical Languages and Pastoral Ministries, as well as a Masters of Divinity from Assemblies of God Theological Seminary. He was privileged to be the Lead Pastor of New Life Assembly in Shillington, PA for four years before suffering sudden paralysis. Jonathan has been a Christian for about 30 years.

His passion is to help imprint the character of Christ through teaching and preaching God's Word. Rev. Jonathan is part of the PennDel Ministry Network. He is a quadriplegic and lives in Central PA with his parents. He enjoys preaching in local churches, writing books, blogging, and answering questions about God and the Bible. He also enjoys reading, watching sports, and geeking out over computers in his "spare" time.

Made in the USA
Monee, IL
07 November 2020

46934015R00046